LUCY THE ELEPHANT®

and

SAMI THE MOUSE

THE BIRTHDAY PARTY

Written by Aunt Evelyn

Illustrated by John Conforti

Printed in the U.S.A.
Published by:
WeBeANS
Galloway Township, NJ

Library of Congress Cataloging-in-Publication Data

Evelyn, Aunt, 1950-
  Lucy the elephant and Sami the mouse : the birthday party / by Aunt Evelyn ; illustrated by John Conforti.
    p. cm.
  Summary: On her birthday, Sami the mouse and her mother take a tour of Lucy, a building shaped like an elephant, who is also celebrating a birthday that day.
  ISBN 0-9740115-1-7 (alk. paper)
  1. Margate Elephant (Hotel)--Juvenile fiction. [1. Margate Elephant (Hotel)--Fiction. 2. Birthdays--Fiction. 3. Mice--Fiction.] I. Title: Birthday party. II. Conforti, John W., 1966- ill. III. Title.
  PZ7.E9117Lu 2004
  [E]--dc22
                          2004013872

Written for my GREAT-nieces and GREAT-nephews:

Alyssa Nicole Armstrong
Ashley Marie Johnson
Aleah Erin Johnson
Ruby Jean Boyer
Annaka Brooke Johnson
Alesha Lee Johnson
Henry Kenneth Boyer
Abby Michele Armstrong
Alec Thomas Armstrong
Cade Michael Spradlin

and children all over the world who love
Lucy the Margate Elephant

Special Thanks to:
Josephine Harron, Co-Founder of The Save Lucy Committee and Chairperson Emeritus,
Richard Helfant, Executive Director,
and all members of the Save Lucy Committee
for their hard work and dedication to Lucy.

One sunny summer morning, little Sami the mouse was having breakfast with her mother, Dee Dee. Dee Dee said to Sami, "Today is July 20th. Do you know why today is a special day?" Sami thought for a few seconds, then said, "Today is my birthday!"

Dee Dee said, "That's right, and today is someone else's birthday, too. We're going to visit our friend, Lucy the Elephant. The people of Margate are having a big birthday party for Lucy, and everyone is invited!"

Sami was very excited to go visit Lucy again, especially for a birthday party! After dressing in their prettiest clothes, Sami and Dee Dee hurried towards Lucy's home on the Margate beach. When they finally saw Lucy, there were already many people at the party.

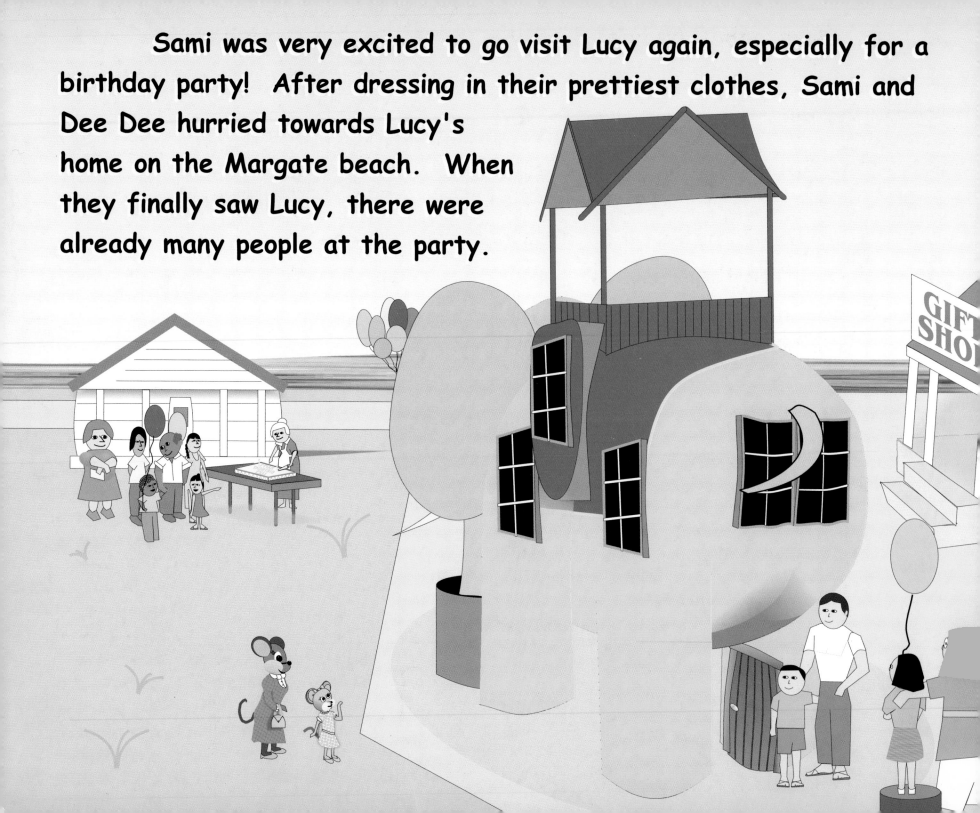

Lucy was happy to see her good friends again. "Hello, Sami and Dee Dee!" she said. "Welcome to my birthday party! Are you going to go on a tour?"

"What's a tour?" asked Sami.

Lucy said, "That's when a person takes you and other visitors for a walk inside my tummy and on my back, and tells you all about me."

Sami was afraid because Lucy was so big, but she was also curious about what she would see inside. So she held her mother's hand real tight, and Tyler the tour guide led them through the door in Lucy's leg and up a round staircase.

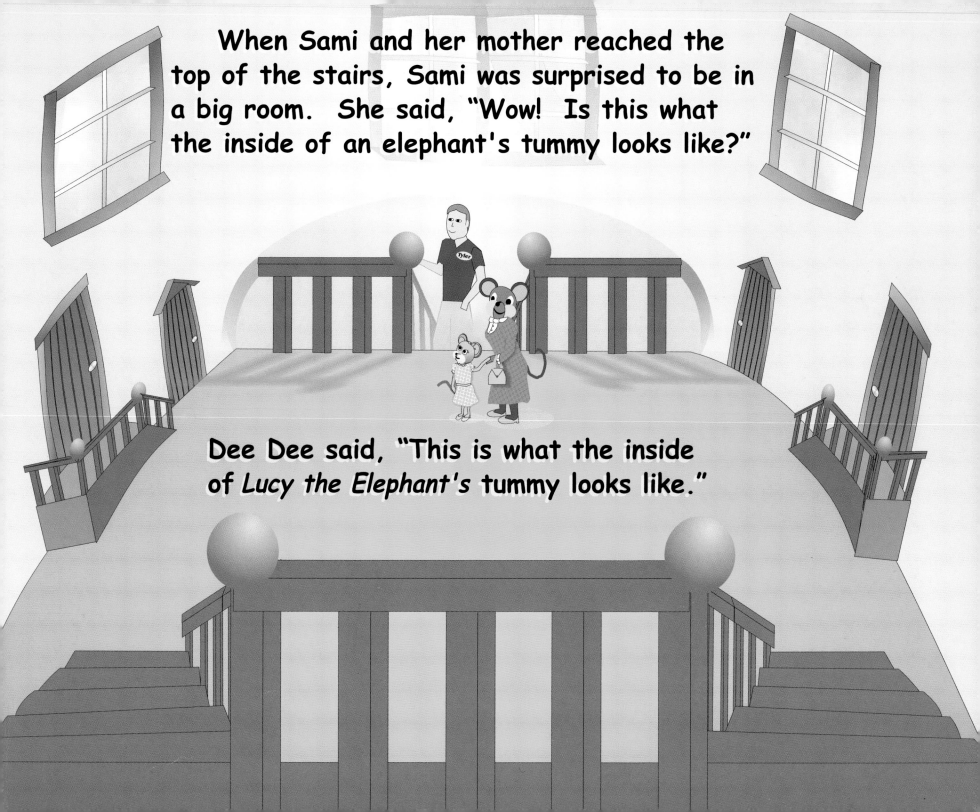

When Sami and her mother reached the top of the stairs, Sami was surprised to be in a big room. She said, "Wow! Is this what the inside of an elephant's tummy looks like?"

Dee Dee said, "This is what the inside of *Lucy the Elephant's* tummy looks like."

At the other side of the room there was a bearded man wearing a suit and a big hat. He said, "My name is Mr. Lafferty. I built this elephant in the year 1881."

Standing next to him was a woman wearing a beautiful long dress. She said, "My name is Sophia Gertzen. When my family bought her from Mr. Lafferty, people just called her The Elephant. I named her Lucy."

Tyler told the visitors, "I'm standing inside Lucy's head. These round windows are Lucy's eyes. You may now come up here and look out of Lucy's eyes. Then you will see what Lucy sees!"

Tyler lifted Sami and Dee Dee so they could see out of Lucy's eye. "Look, Mommy!" Sami said to Dee Dee. "I see the Atlantic Ocean! I see boats! And dolphins!"

Dee Dee said, "Lucy also sees the sun come up over the ocean every day. She's very lucky! And we're lucky to have Lucy here in our little town of Margate."

Then Tyler took the visitors up another round staircase onto Lucy's back. Tyler said, "In a country called India, far, far away, people ride on the backs of real elephants in a seat called a howdah.* Right now, we're in Lucy's howdah."

They were so high up in the air they could see many miles away, past Margate to the tall buildings of Atlantic City. They stayed on the howdah for a couple of minutes enjoying the view, then they walked down the stairs.

Myra's

Eunice's

* pronounced HOW'duh

Back on the ground where they had started the tour, Tyler said, "Let's all sing Happy Birthday to Lucy."

Suddenly, they heard a loud voice coming from Lucy! The voice said, "Wait! It's also my friend Sami's birthday." The visitors couldn't believe what they heard--it was *Lucy* talking to them!

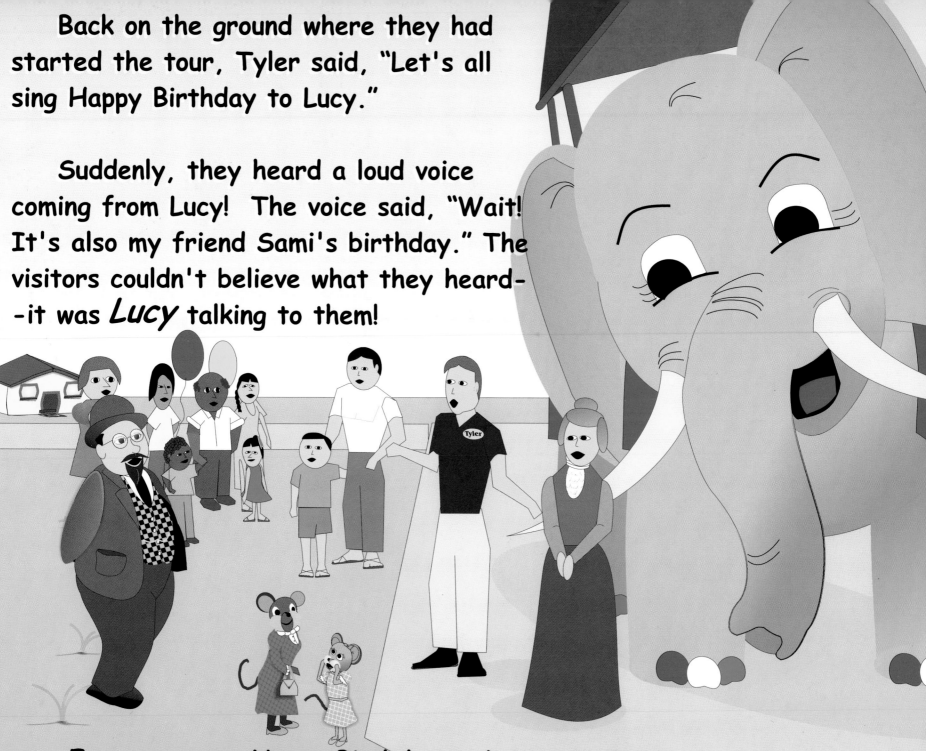

Everyone sang Happy Birthday to Lucy *and* Sami.

Sami didn't want the day to end. She said, "Going on a tour inside Lucy was fun! Is my birthday over now?" Dee Dee said, "No, we're going to go have your favorite dessert - cheesecake." Sami said, "Thank you, Mommy. This has been the best birthday *ever!*"

As they started to walk away, Sami turned around and said to Lucy, "Happy Birthday, Lucy! I'll be back to see you again soon."

Lucy smiled and winked at Sami, and whispered, "Happy birthday, little mouse."

Photo courtesy of the Save Lucy Committee.

READERS:

Lucy the Margate Elephant was built in 1881 by James Lafferty of Philadelphia, as his real estate office. He sold it in 1887 to Anthony Gertzen. In 1969, the Gertzen family sold the land Lucy was on, and gave Lucy to the Save Lucy Committee. The Save Lucy Committee raised the money needed to move Lucy to her new home two blocks away, which was provided by Margate City. Moving day was July 20, 1970. Lucy's birthday is now celebrated on July 20th every year.

About the Author

Evelyn (Stout) Johnson, originally from Washington, D.C., graduated from Northwestern High School in Hyattsville, Maryland, attended Abilene Christian University in Abilene, Texas, and holds an Associate Degree in Human Services from Northern Virginia Community College. Evelyn worked as a secretary her entire adult life until 2000, when she and her husband moved to their house in Ocean City, NJ.

While scanning the want ads for a summer job, she saw one that captured her interest: "Tour guides wanted for Lucy the Elephant." She applied for the job and was hired. Evelyn is currently Lucy's Tour Director.

Evelyn noticed that many young children were afraid of Lucy, so she wrote a bedtime story to show Lucy as nothing to fear. She used the names of real tour guides for characters in the book. Sami the Mouse is named after Samantha Nigro. Dee Dee, Sami's mother, is named after Danielle Principato. In The Birthday Party, Tyler is Tyler Francz.

Some time after Evelyn wrote the first book, she was browsing in Lucy's website and saw a drawing of Lucy. John Conforti, the artist behind the drawing, was also the webmaster for Lucy. They agreed to collaborate to produce "Lucy the Elephant and Sami the Mouse." Evelyn says, "John has taken the ideas for my story and created the vivid images all young children crave. It turned out better than I imagined it could! Without John's artistic ability, his publishing knowledge, and his persistence, I don't know if my book would have ever been published."

About the Illustrator

John Conforti is a graduate of the George Washington University in Washington, D.C., where he earned degrees in Art, Music, Drama and Communications. He is CEO and Lead Designer of his own company, WeBeANS, which specializes in the digital arts. He currently resides in New Jersey with his wife of ten years and his two children.

Our deepest gratitude to Myra and George Hyman & Eunice and David Sherwood for their generous sponsorship of this book.

Look for the ORIGINAL "Lucy the Elephant and Sami the Mouse" at www.lucytheelephant.org